Ser~

Captain Chunder

Save The Day Again

JAMES SHARKEY

Chunder
&
Smelly

www.sergeantsmelly.co.uk

Other titles by James Sharkey
Sergeant Smelly And Captain Chunder Save The Day
Sergeant Smelly And Captain Chunder: Lost in Time
Sergeant Smelly And Captain Chunder: Dimensions
A Sergeant Smelly Christmas
Sergeant Smelly And Captain Chunder: Aliens

Sergeant Smelly And Captain Chunder Save The Day
Audio book

To Connor again

And John

1 RISE OF THE ONION

Onionman stared at the cold, damp wall of the cave. He knew every inch, every twist and turn, every nook and cranny. Hours spent watching the creation of every spider web. Engineering wonders he could only dream of building. Time passed slowly since his defeat at the hands of Sergeant Smelly and Captain Chunder. Or should I say, at the bottom of Sergeant Smelly. Six long, dull months trapped in a cave with Bunion Man.

Bunion Man was a failed evil villain who attempted to inflict pain on bunion sufferers, but his efforts were a disastrous failure, as he was completely and utterly devoid of evil. He was the world's second most awful evil villain that ever lived. Only beaten in the awful stakes by Super Snale, who was not only terrible at spelling, but the world's slowest evil villain too. The only evil thing he ever did was leave a particularly nasty slime that took forever to get off the bottom of your shoe.

Onionman spent six months in the cave so everyone would think he was dead, but all this time was spent planning his revenge.

As much as he hated him, Bunion Man's plan was far superior than any of his own over the last six months.

One dark and dismal day, as days in caves tend to be, Bunion Man said to Onionman, "Why don't you branch out and have other evil vegetables rather than just onions?"

"Oh shut up Bunion Man…no wait…that's it Bunion Man. You are a genius…okay, you are maybe not a genius, but that is an excellent idea," said Onionman.

"As it was such a good idea, can I be a part of your evil organisation?" asked Bunion Man with a ridiculous grin on his face.

"No, don't be preposterous. Onionman and Bunion Man is wrong on so many levels! Like farting in an elevator."

Onionman's new evil plot to rule the world had begun.

2 BACK AT CAFÉ MCPOO

Meanwhile back at Café McPoo, Sergeant Smelly was bragging about his superhero escapades with epic tales of how he defeated Onionman. Forgetting to mention Captain Chunder of course, who was busy in the kitchen doing what he did best. No, not puking. He was creating culinary delights such as Pickled Egg and Chilli Pizza and Brussels Sprouts Bruschetta. Fame did not interest him in the slightest. He was happiest in the kitchen creating gorgeous gourmet grub for his customers.

Sergeant Smelly loved his new superhero status and his popularity was soaring, with over a million cartoon facebook friends. He didn't read it much though, as he didn't care about looking at photos of what people were eating or what they thought about the TV programmes they were watching. And he didn't like those Elfie things where people got dressed up as an Elf and took a photo of themselves.

People would crowd around him in the restaurant to hear him speak of his courageous battles with Onionman and smell his farts. People do the most bizarre things when famous people are involved. He even sold signed photos of his fartastic fire-farts, but he secretly hoped there would be no more evil villains and Onionman would not return with more world domination plans. It wasn't because he was scared. No, he was enjoying the attention so much, he didn't want it to stop. Okay, maybe he was a little scared, but he didn't tell anyone. He gave up his job as a Sergeant in the army and he was earning pot loads of cash from appearing in magazines and TV interviews. But why they gave him the cash in pots was beyond him. His pot collection was remarkable. They even made a ride at a theme park called The Fire-Fart Express and Sergeant Smelly merchandise could be bought throughout the park. He didn't want the fame and fortune to end. But trouble was brewing in Café McPoo.

3 PUMPKIN PIE

Johnny Pumpkin walked into Café McPoo with high expectations. He recently read a review of the Pumpkin Pie and was eager to taste it. He loved food from an early age, but in particular, he craved Pumpkin Pie.

"Farting or Non-Farting?" asked the waitress to Johnny Pumpkin as he entered

Café McPoo. Johnny knew this was coming, as he had read an interview with Sergeant Smelly about the first time he visited Café McPoo.

"Non-Farting please." He went for the Non Farting section where he was on his own. He was only there for the Pumpkin Pie after all. He wasn't fussy about getting a signed fire-fart photo from Sergeant Smelly. The waitress handed him the menu and he ordered the Pumpkin Pie.

"I'll have the Pumpkin Pie please waitress," said Johnny Pumpkin with a huge grin on his face.

"With or without extra hot chilli sauce?"

"Oh definitely without please. I don't have the strongest of bottoms thank you very much."

"That's too much information thank YOU very much," said the waitress rolling her eyes as she walked off with Johnny Pumpkin's order. The waitress returned a few minutes later with the heavenly dish and the glorious smell of pumpkin drifted up his nostrils. He was happy as Larry McLarry, the happy man who lived across the street from him. He stared at the pie intently, breathing in the appetizing aroma before tucking into the pie. It was so delicious, he ate it all in less than a minute. It was the most glorious food he had ever eaten. The pie seemed spicy as he ate it, but the chilli effect was only now starting to come back on him. His face reddened and his mouth began to burn. His eyes grew wider and wider and his face was now a shade of burning hot red. Smoke started to puff out of his ears. He was aboard the Extra Hot Chilli Express on its way to chilli oblivion. An Extra Hot Chilli Express with no brakes and on a collision course with a ring of fire.

"WAITRESS!!!" screamed Johnny Pumpkin. "WHAT ON EARTH HAVE YOU DONE TO ME? I DON'T REMEMBER ASKING YOU TO PUT RED HOT LAVA IN MY PUMPKIN PIE."

The waitress opened her mouth to reply, when she heard another yell.

"WAITRESS!!!" shouted Sergeant Smelly. "HOW AM I SUPPOSED TO PRODUCE MY FIRE-FARTS WITH THIS NON SPICY DRIVEL!"

Her heart sank as she realised the mistake. The orders were mixed up and Johnny Pumpkin ate Sergeant Smelly's dish, which was Pumpkin Pie with extra hot Chilli Sauce, also known as THE FIRE-FARTER.

"Oh Pumping Pumpkins," said the waitress as she panicked and ran over to Johnny Pumpkin's table and grabbed his empty dish. She ran over to Sergeant Smelly's table and switched the dishes, not realising one was empty. She rushed to the kitchen and came back with a cold glass of milk for him.

"Please accept my most humble apologies Sir," said the waitress apologising for her error. Johnny Pumpkin grabbed the milk and poured it down his throat, splashing the milk all over his face and clothes, but his face was still red and his throat was on fire.

"What on earth are you trying to do to me?" shrieked Johnny Pumpkin at the top of his voice.

"I'm sorry Sir, if you tell me your name I will book you a table for next week and you'll get a free meal," replied the waitress.

"My name is…"

The commotion caused all the customers to listen to the conversation.

"My name is…"

You could hear a pin drop, but that was due to the strange man in the corner dropping heavy pins into a metal basin. The waitress shouted, "Can you stop dropping those heavy pins into the metal basin for no apparent reason please? We are trying to hear his name."

"MY NAME IS JOHNNY PUMPKIN."

Silence engulfed the café and everyone stared at Johnny Pumpkin.

"No seriously," said the waitress. "What is your name?"

Johnny Pumpkin grew madder and madder as his throat was still on fire.

"MY NAME IS JOHNNY PUMPKIN!"

Another short silence was followed by howls of laughter.

"WHAT ARE YOU LAUGHING AT YOU MORONS?" shouted Johnny Pumpkin who couldn't understand why they were laughing at him.

"You've burned your throat eating Pumpkin Pie with extra hot Chilli sauce and your name is Johnny Pumpkin," said one of the customers in the restaurant, which led to another round of laughter at Johnny Pumpkin's expense.

And then it hit him. He felt a rumbling in his tummy which led down to his bottom and without any further warning, a fire-fart ripped from his buttocks tearing his trousers and setting the tablecloth on fire. His chair flew backwards and he fell off his chair. This led to another round of giggling and rolling about the floor. His trousers were ruined and he bought them especially for his visit to Café McPoo.

"We'll have to rename the dish PUMPING PUMPKIN PIE now," shrieked Sergeant Smelly. The café erupted into fits of laughter again.

Johnny Pumpkin ran out of Café McPoo totally embarrassed and downhearted. His elation of visiting Café McPoo turned to sorrow in an instant. From that day forward he vowed he would destroy Sergeant Smelly and his superhero reputation if it was the last thing he did. A silly vow to make, because if it was the last thing he ever did, he wouldn't be able to savour his revenge. But he said it anyway and he wasn't a man to go back on his word.

4 JOHNNY PUMPKIN'S REVENGE

Johnny Pumpkin reached his house in the nick of time and he rushed to the toilet. He was a sad and smelly man. Not to mention a sore bottomed man. He smelled like ten rotten eggs had been smeared all over him with boiled cabbage leaves. Sergeant Smelly had humiliated him

and he was out for revenge, as well as a
shower.

He racked his brains for hours but could
not think of a suitable revenge. His bottom
did not help matters, as every so often, he
would produce a putrid pump that made
him nauseous. He walked painfully into the
shower and cleaned himself up. He didn't
want to ruin another pair of trousers, so sat
plotting in his pants. I said PLOTTING!

But things were about to get even worse
for Johnny Pumpkin. He lay in his bed and
eventually fell asleep once the pain in his
bottom had eased. He wandered off into a
dream. A dream which started off pleasantly
but slowly descended into a nightmare. He
was back at Café McPoo, but this time the
waitress served him the correct order and

the pie was equally as good as he hoped. So good in fact, he ordered another one, but then the nightmare began and everyone laughed at him and pointed at his head. He looked in the mirror and saw his head had transmogrified into a huge pumpkin.

"CURSE YOU SERGEANT SMELLY!" he shouted in his dream as he fell to his knees with his giant pumpkin head in his hands.

He awoke the next morning with a thumping sore head and an extremely sore bottom. He crawled through to the bathroom and slowly dragged himself up to the sink. He gradually opened his eyes in front of the mirror. His eyes widened in slow motion as he could not believe what he was seeing. He rubbed his eyes to make sure he wasn't still dreaming. But this was no dream. It was a living nightmare. A giant pumpkin sat in the same spot where his head used to be. The usual facial features were still present, but were now two triangular eyes and a crooked smile shaped like a bat with lightning for wings.

"WHAT THE PUMPING PUMPKINS HAS HAPPENED TO ME!" shrieked Johnny Pumpkin. He immediately thought of the teasing he would get.

"Is it Halloween already pumpkin head?" shouted funny person 1.

"He's got a pumpkin for a head, he's got a pumpkin for a head," sang funny person 2.

"What do you call 3.14 pumpkins? Pumpkin Pi," said funny person 3.

People would upload his photo to facebook and mock him.

He could only hope no one had recorded the incident at the café. Desperation dragged him to his knees and he screamed at the top of his voice, "I WILL GET MY REVENGE ON YOU SERGEANT SMELLY!"

And as so often happens immediately after having a revengeful moment of clarity, the doorbell rang.

5 EVIL VEGETABLES

Johnny Pumpkin opened the door to a strange sight which reminded him of his nightmare.

"Hi, I'm Onionman. And going by the pumpkin you have for a head and the awful pong in your house, I assume you must be Smelly Vegetable Man," said Onionman who was dreadful at naming things.

"WHAT? Is it Halloween already? Who are you?"

"Seriously?" enquired Onionman. "You have a gigantic pumpkin for a head and you are asking ME if it's Halloween?"

"Look, I've had a bad couple of days…"

"It is Halloween by the way," interrupted Onionman.

"Oh shut up," snapped Johnny Pumpkin. "I'm not in the mood for…"

"I'm just saying," interrupted Onionman again.

"Well just don't say. Don't say anything. Who are you and what do you want?"

The silence lasted for five minutes before Johnny Pumpkin could take no more.

"Yes, okay, I know I said don't say anything, but you can tell me who you are and what it is you want."

"I AM ONIONMAN. I WANT WORLD DOMINATION," said Onionman in capital letters to show how important he was. "And I think I can help you," he added mischievously.

"How can you help me? I don't know you and you don't know me," replied Johnny Pumpkin getting more confused and angry by the second.

"On the contrary my dear Pumpkin. I know you don't like Sergeant Smelly because I saw you on YouTube."

"Don't call me a tube you evil onion man!"

"Ah, so you do know who I am after all," said Onionman.

" I didn't, but I put two and two together and guessed your name."

"But my name isn't Four!"

"WHAT? Stop being ridiculous."

"I can't. I'm evil. I have to be ridiculous."

"So why did you call me a tube?"

"I didn't. I saw you on the internet on YouTube. It's a website where people can upload embarrassing videos. Someone recorded your awful, yet highly amusing experience at Café McPoo yesterday and posted it on YouTube. It has reached a million hits already. You are a viral star."

"What on earth is a viral star? Is that the one next to Uranus?" a bemused Johnny Pumpkin replied.

"I have no idea, but you have become famous because a million people have watched and shared the video. Here, I'll show you on my oPad."

"What is an oPad?"

"Really Smelly Vegetable Man. You must keep up with the times. It is an onion pad and I can go on the internet and watch videos of people making a fool of themselves."

"That looks like a tablet with a picture of an onion stuck on the back. And my name is Johnny Pumpkin."

"Seriously…your name actually is Johnny Pumpkin. Whatever, here, watch the video."

Onionman handed the badly constructed oPad to Johnny Pumpkin and he sunk to his knees in horror.

"CURSE YOU SERGEANT SMELLY! I WILL HAVE MY REVENGE, YOU ANNOYING FIRE-FARTING SUPERHERO," bawled Johnny Pumpkin still on his knees for dramatic effect. And he sobbed uncontrollably for thirty minutes.

6 THE PLAN

Once Johnny Pumpkin had finished sobbing uncontrollably, Onionman continued, "So, are you calm enough to talk about your revenge on Sergeant Smelly yet?" asked Onionman.

"Yes, I'm fine now. What were you saying?"

"Was it the bit about you being a viral star?"

"No, the bit about revenge on Sergeant Smelly and world domination," said Johnny Pumpkin. "And what is it with you and this world domination thing anyway?"

"I like to dominate things. Things like the world and stuff," replied Onionman.

"Have you ever dominated the world before? Have you ever dominated anything?"

"Yes, I was well on my way to world domination when Sergeant Smelly stuck his fat, smelly, fire-farting butt in. I dominated London. So actually Johnny Pumpkin, yes, I have dominated something. How do you like dem apples?"

"What apples?" Johnny Pumpkin looked perplexed.

"Those apples in your fruit bowl. They look nice."

"Err…yes, they are lovely apples and I like dem. Anyhoos, you didn't dominate the world did you, so you don't know if you actually like it or not? And it never works anyway. Haven't you watched any James Bond films? The evil villains hell-bent on world domination usually end up getting eaten by sharks or badly injured when their inventions go wrong. They also never get rid of the hero when they get the chance. They entrust the job of doing away with the hero to the man who started evil villainry training a week ago and doesn't have any experience in disposing of heroes. Do you know what I mean Onionman?" ranted Johnny Pumpkin.

"No, I've never heard of James Bond."

"How strange! Anyway, how can you help me get my revenge on Sergeant Smelly?" asked Johnny Pumpkin.

"We have an ingenious plan," replied Onionman.

"What is it?" enquired Johnny Pumpkin.

"It is a cunning proposed course of action," replied Onionman.

"I know what the definition of an ingenious plan is, but what is your actual plan?" enquired Johnny Pumpkin again.

"Oh I don't know what the plan is. I haven't come up with the actual plan yet. I was hoping you would help me with it," said Onionman.

"Soooo…when you said you could help me, what you really meant is you want ME to help YOU!" said Johnny Pumpkin raising his voice.

"Yes. Ingenious isn't it?"

A huge pause followed. It wasn't an awkward silence, more of a stupendously dumbstruck silence from Johnny Pumpkin as he could not believe what was happening. "Soooo…what is the plan Johnny Pumpkin?" asked Onionman annoyingly.

"You actually want me to come up with an ingenious plan right this minute."

"Yes please."

"Well, perhaps we can have a random chapter to give me time to think."

And with that, a random chapter was randomly created to give Johnny Pumpkin time to think of an ingenious plan.

7 RANDOM CHAPTER 1

Meanwhile, back at the cave, Bunion Man was bored of being a failed evil villain nobody knew and annoyed that Onionman did not treat him as an equal. He had some serious thinking to do. His first idea was to go back to evil villainry school and work harder this time, instead of playing video games and watching YouTube videos about random people playing video games. This time he would actually read the books on the reading list;

- ☞ How to Defeat Farting Superheroes
- ☞ How to Leave Inexperienced Staff to Dispose of Superheroes
- ☞ How to Laugh Evilly
- ☞ How to Produce Evil Laughs Without Getting a Sore Throat
- ☞ The Dummies Guide to Evil Planning

The second idea was to wreak revenge on Onionman and foil his attempts at world domination, but he didn't have any foil. He was undecided where his loyalties would lie.

8 THE ACTUAL PLAN

One random chapter later and Onionman was as impatient as ever.

"Soooo…what is the plan Johnny Pumpkin?" repeated Onionman.

"Do you think the random chapter that was randomly created to give me a chance to think of an ingenious plan was enough time?" asked Johnny Pumpkin.

"I certainly hope so. It has been literally minutes since the random chapter. How much time or random chapters do you need?" enquired Onionman getting irritated with Johnny Pumpkin's inability to come up with an ingenious plan within the time constraints of the random chapter.

"Well, actually, I do have an ingenious plan," said Johnny Pumpkin.

"Is it ingenious?" asked Onionman excitedly.

"What? Is the ingenious plan ingenious? Well yes, Sherlock! Yes it is ingenious," said Johnny Pumpkin.

"Who is Sherlock?" enquired Onionman.

"He is my friend who is sitting behind you. Sherlock McRandom meet Onionman. Onionman meet Sherlock McRandom."

"Hi, large oddly shaped onion," said Sherlock McRandom randomly.

"Err...hi Sherlock," said Onionman.

"Soooo...can you tell me what the plan is please?" pleaded Onionman again.

"US," exclaimed Johnny Pumpkin.

"What? US? That's the plan...US!"

"No, can you tell US what the plan is," replied Johnny Pumpkin pointing to himself and Sherlock McRandom.

"Of course I can't tell you the plan. I DON'T KNOW IT!" barked Onionman getting frustrated and confused.

"Relax Onionman and I will tell you what the plan is."

"Good," said Onionman who was getting exasperated. "I'm getting exasperated here and I don't even know what it means! Please, please, pretty please with crispy diced onions and bacon on top. Tell me what the plan is."

"Well, actually, I don't have an ingenious plan."

"WHAT…ARRRGGHHH!" yelled Onionman.

"Wait Onionman. I don't have an ingenious plan…I have an EVIL ingenious plan," said Johnny Pumpkin.

"Ahh…I see what you did there. So what is the EVIL ingenious plan then?"

"When I was at the restaurant, Sergeant Smelly was signing his recipe book. We should make it into an e-book and post it online for free. Millions of people will download it because it is free. Everybody likes something for free!"

"Especially if they don't have to pay for it," Onionman interrupted stupidly.

"Err...yes. Anyhoos, as I was saying before I was stupidly interrupted. Millions of people all over the world will cook Captain Chunder's recipes which will have the same effect as cows eating too much and being in a constant state of fartdom."

"I'm not sure I follow you Johnny Pumpkin," said Onionman not being able to follow Johnny Pumpkin.

"I'm not surprised Onionman. I'm not on twitter yet and I don't have a blog. Maybe after the book comes out though. Who knows! Anyhoos, the cows being in a constant state of fartdom helps to destroy the ozone layer, so if everyone eats fart inducing recipes, the hole in the ozone layer will increase."

"I still don't follow you," said Onionman still unable to follow Johnny Pumpkin.

"I'm not surprised Onionman, it has only been a few sentences and I still don't have a twitter account or a blog. I'll let you know when everything is up and running and you can follow me. Now shut up and pay attention. If the hole in the ozone layer increases, it will have a dramatic effect on the world's climate and cause a major disaster."

"Ooh, ooh, I know Major Disaster. He tried to prevent a major disaster, namely me, but failed muchly."

"Err…indeed. So we blame the major disaster on Sergeant Smelly and his book. We will say he did it on porpoise and he will be put in prison for destroying the ozone layer."

"On porpoise? Isn't that a dolphin? We can't blame the dolphins. They are lovely animals with all their eeking and clicking and stuff. Even I'm not that evil!"

"Sorry, I meant, we will say he did it on purpose," said Johnny Pumpkin correcting himself.

"And what about Major Disaster?" enquired Onionman.

"What? Yes, okay Onionman, we can blame Major Disaster for the major disaster as well, if it makes you happy."

"Yay!" exclaimed Onionman. "But before we put this plan into action, we will have to give you an evil villain name."

"Will we require another random chapter to give us time to think?"

"No, a short chapter should do the trick."

9 NAMING THE NEW EVIL VILLAIN

Onionman began the evil villain naming ceremony with one of his usual awful names.

"What about Smelly Vegetable Man?"

"No, you said that already. And I don't even smell that bad."

"Seriously, you think you don't smell that bad. This room smells worse than boiled cabbage mixed with rotten eggs!"

"Oh be quiet Onionman. Right let's think about this in a list.

- I'm EVIL
- I can't stop PUMPING
- I have a PUMPKIN for a head
- I am a MAN

So, to summarise;

- EVIL
- PUMPING
- PUMPKIN
- MAN

"I'VE GOT IT, WHAT ABOUT THE EVIL PUMPKIN MAN WHO PUMPS A LOT!" shouted Onionman with a eureka moment.

"Seriously! I give you all that and you give me THE EVIL PUMPKIN MAN WHO PUMPS A LOT. Cheesy Pumpkin Pies. You are appalling at naming things aren't you. So, again…to summarise…slowly;

- EVIL
- PUMPING
- PUMPKIN
- MAN

So, what are you thinking now Onionman. Please tell me you have got it this time?" said Johnny Pumpkin.

"Steve?"

10 PLAN IN ACTION

After Johnny Pumpkin explained to Onionman his new evil name would be Evil Pumping Pumpkin Man and not Steve, the evil ingenious plan was put in motion.

They set up a website called www.freeawesomerecipes.com to post the recipes from Sergeant Smelly's book.

Onionman went to the book store to buy a copy of Sergeant Smelly's Recipes From Café McPoo. Unfortunately, he didn't notice the book signing taking place. He joined what he thought was the queue for the till, but when he reached the front, Sergeant Smelly was waiting to sign his book.

"ARRRGGGH!" screamed Sergeant Smelly. "IT'S ONIONMAN!"

"Err…no…it's not me Sergeant Smelly. It's Halloween and I am merely dressed like Onionman," said Onionman thinking on his feet. He didn't usually think on his feet. He usually liked thinking on his arms, but the time for thinking on his arms was not now. Now was the time for thinking on his feet. Which he did.

"Err…yes, yes, yes, of course," stuttered Sergeant Smelly pretending not to be scared. "I knew all along it wasn't Onionman. I was pretending to be scared but I am actually fearless," he continued lying through his teeth. He didn't usually lie through his teeth. He usually liked lying through his ears, but the time for lying through his ears was not now. Now was the time for lying through his teeth. Which he did.

"Yeah right," whispered Onionman, aware that Sergeant Smelly was lying through his teeth.

"Sorry, what did you say, person dressed as Onionman who definitely isn't Onionman?" asked Sergeant Smelly to the person he thought was dressed as Onionman.

"I said, yeah, that's right, you are fearless. Thank you for saving the day from the cunningly evil Onionman," seethed Onionman trying to hide his anger. Sergeant Smelly signed the book and Onionman left the shop in a hurry.

"What took you so long?" asked Evil Pumping Pumpkin Man.

"I bumped into Sergeant Smelly and he signed the book," replied Onionman.

"Excellent idea, we can use his signature and put it on the website. Didn't he recognise you?" enquired Evil Pumping Pumpkin Man.

"Yes, but I told him I was dressed up for Halloween," replied Onionman with a smug grin on his face.

"But it's July. Halloween is months away."

"Err, oh yeah…but I knew Sergeant Smelly would fall for it anyway," lied Onionman.

"Well, never mind that now, let's get to work uploading the free recipes that will destroy Sergeant Smelly's superhero reputation."

They uploaded the free book to the website and set up a cartoon facebook campaign that directed everyone to their website. They also did a twittery thing that received thousands of followers, but Onionman didn't understand what the twittery thing would do.

"I'm not sure I want loads of people following me around everywhere," he said bewildered.

Soon millions of people around the world downloaded the book free of charge and made the recipes. Within a week, 10% of the world's population had cooked Captain Chunder's fart inducing recipes, but major disaster was not around the corner. It was general disarray who was around the corner.

"Morning, evil bad doers," said General Disarray.

They had only created general disarray, but were hoping for a major disaster.

11 FRAMED

Back at Café McPoo, Sergeant Smelly was on the internet googling himself when he came across a worrying news story.

"Have you looked at the internet today Captain Chunder," asked Sergeant Smelly in shock.

"No, I don't do the internet much to be honest," replied Captain Chunder. "I preferred the days when the news was read out to me on TV without people commenting on it. I don't care what Andy from Bristol has to say about oil prices. I'm not interested in having pretend friends or being invited to play games I don't want…"

"Bored," interrupted Sergeant Smelly rather rudely. "Someone has taken your recipes…" said Sergeant Smelly, but was quickly interrupted by Captain Chunder.

"You mean the recipes you stole from me and made into a book!"

"Yes those ones. But now isn't the time to be bitter, Captain Chunder. The recipes are available to download free! It's also on the news that this could have an effect on the hole in the ozone layer. It's increasing because everyone is eating the fart inducing recipes and unless everyone stops farting, we are all faced with a foul-smelling impending doom. But more importantly, sales of my book have plummeted due to everyone downloading it for free. That can't be fair or legal can it?" asked Sergeant Smelly.

"WHAT?" shouted Captain Chunder.

"You surely don't want me to repeat all that again do you Chunder?" said Sergeant Smelly.

"No, you didn't let me finish, WHAT…was the middle bit again?"

"Was it the bit about being unfair because sales in my book have plummeted due to everyone downloading it for free?" asked Sergeant Smelly.

"No, the bit that wasn't about you, Smelly?" said Captain Chunder impatiently.

"Oh, you mean the bit about the hole in the ozone layer increasing and unless everyone stops farting, we are all faced with a foul-smelling impending doom."

"Yes, that bit."

"The hole in the ozone layer is increasing and unless everyone stops farting, we are all faced with a foul-smelling impending doom," repeated Sergeant Smelly.

"Don't you think that is important? Don't you think it's way more important than you making less money from the recipes you stole from ME!" shouted Captain Chunder.

"Okay, if you put it that way. And if we get the impending doom thing, no one will be able to buy my books," continued Sergeant Smelly still being selfish. "Ah yes, I see what you mean now Chunder."

"Exactly!" said Captain Chunder. "Well, no, not exactly. I was thinking how the impending doom would affect everyone in the world, rather than how it would affect their ability to buy your book," said Captain Chunder, sadly realising he wasn't getting through to Sergeant Smelly.

"What is impending doom anyway?" asked Sergeant Smelly oblivious to the point Captain Chunder was trying to make. "I thought Impending Doom was a rock band from London."

"For most people it will mean a major disaster and the world could end. For you it means less sales of the book that should have been mine," said Captain Chunder.

"Ah! so I was right all along!" said Sergeant Smelly.

"Let me see the website," said Captain Chunder hoping Sergeant Smelly wasn't getting his facts right. He didn't do too badly and he got most of them right. Apart from the most important part of course.

"Sergeant Smelly, you didn't read the entire story. It says this could have an effect on the hole in the ozone layer…

…in the next fifty years!"

"Ah, so we just have to get their website shut down and everyone will buy my book again and we can let Son of Sergeant Smelly and Son of Captain Chunder save the day."

"Yes, WHAT...NO. You are missing the point Sergeant Smelly. We need to do something right now, but the doom isn't impending anymore. It's more long range doom, rather than impending doom. We have to do something to sort this out. Who could possibly be behind this dastardly deed Sergeant Smelly?" asked Captain Chunder. "Hmm...are you thinking what I am thinking Sergeant Smelly?" Captain Chunder continued.

"Are you thinking about a Haggis, Pepperoni and Baked Bean Pie?" enquired Sergeant Smelly.

"No."

"Are you thinking about a fifteen inch Pepperoni, Egg and Chilli pizza?" enquired Sergeant Smelly.

"No."

"Then no, I am not thinking what you are thinking, as you're thinking I'm thinking what you're thinking," replied Sergeant Smelly.

"I'll give you a clue Sergeant Smelly…onions."

"I've got it…Pepperoni, Egg, Chilli and Onion Pizza!" exclaimed Sergeant Smelly triumphantly again.

"No, you smelly idiot. I mean Onionman, our arch nemesis."

"Of course," lied Sergeant Smelly. "That was my next thought after the pizza."

"Sergeant Smelly. I'm afraid it's time to be a superhero again."

"Oh dear," groaned Sergeant Smelly.

12 RETHINK

As news filtered through that it might take longer than expected for the major disaster to occur, Onionman was having his doubts.

" I don't think your plan is working Evil Pumping Pumpkin Man," said Onionman.

"Worry not Onionman. I did not tell you the entire plan in case you didn't understand," said Evil Pumping Pumpkin Man slightly patronising Onionman.

"Butt…butt…butt…" stuttered Onionman, "I mean but…but…but…" stuttered Onionman. "What do you mean? I am an evil genius. I would have fully understood your plan!" replied Onionman feeling insulted. "Tell me what the rest of the plan is or I won't let you use my evil hench-onions Who or whom …"

"You have evil hench-onions called Who and Whom? Why?"

"No, I hadn't finished. Who or whom will now be called my monions."

"Soooo…the onions called Who or Whom will now be called monions!" said Evil Pumping Pumpkin Man confused.

"No, I'm never sure when to use Who or Whom so I said Who or Whom. Most of my hench-onions, sorry, monions are called Onion with a number after the Onion. Onion 324 for example. And Onion 324 will now be called Monion 324."

"Doesn't that get confusing? You said most of them. What are the rest of them called?"

"It can be confusing sometimes. One of them is called Onion Bob. He wanted be called Onion Bob instead of his previous name of Unlucky Onion 7. Anyhoos, tell me what the rest of the plan is please."

"Well, I had a back-up plan if the farting thing didn't work. It probably is working, but we might have to wait fifty years or so. I built a machine that creates a hole in the ozone layer."

"Ooh, ooh, ooh. Can I name it? Can I name it? Please, please, pretty please with fried onions and garlic mushrooms on top, please."

"But I have already named it. It is called DEATH TO THE OZONE! Poo ha ha ha ha," laughed Evil Pumping Pumpkin Man, trying out his new evil laugh. Onionman looked at him with pity in his eyes. "Seriously, that is one awful name!"

Evil Pumping Pumpkin Man recently found out how bad at naming things Onionman was, but he was about to be reminded.

Evil Pumping Pumpkin Man hadn't been to the Evil school of Villainry and went for the conventional practical naming choices. If he had gone to the Evil school of Villainry, he would have known how bad Onionman was in the class for Naming Evil Inventions.

He got an A+ when he created a Time Machine in the Evil Inventions class, but he got a Z- when he named it The Machine that puts you back in time then brings you back to the present once you have finished distorting the Space Time Continuum.

"I think it should be called, The Machine that puts a hole in the ozone layer and destroys Sergeant Smelly's reputation. Well, what do ya think about that Evil Pumpy Man?"

"Seriously, you think The Machine that puts a hole in the ozone layer and destroys

Sergeant Smelly's reputation is better than DEATH TO THE OZONE?"

"Yes. Yes I do."

"Well, it does have a certain ring to it." The sarcasm was standing upright in Onionman's face, but once again he was oblivious to it.

"It does, doesn't it?" replied Onionman.

"No Onionman, I was being sarcastic," said Evil Pumping Pumpkin Man.

"So can we change it?" replied Onionman.

Evil Pumping Pumpkin Man paused to think for a second. A grin appeared on his face as he said, "On one condition."

"Okay."

"If I rename it, you have to press the button that fires the laser that creates a hole in the ozone layer."

"That's your condition. Of course I'll do it. I assumed it was my job anyway."

"Done, The Machine that puts a hole in the ozone layer and destroys Sergeant Smelly's reputation it is. I did mention you have to fly to space in a rocket that I recently built and press the button didn't I?" said Evil Pumping Pumpkin Man.

"Err...no, you most certainly didn't but that's even more awesome. You just keep on giving, Pumpy," said Onionman getting carried away.

"Put me down you silly monions," he said to the monions who were carrying him away.

"Excellent," said Evil Pumping Pumpkin Man as he got to work setting up The

Machine that puts a hole in the ozone layer and destroys Sergeant Smelly's reputation.

Onionman also tried to change the name of the button, but Evil Pumping Pumpkin Man was having none of it. He almost called the button Death to the Ozone and almost certain death to the presser of the button, but decided on a last minute change in case Onionman understood what the button actually did.

13 BRAINSTORMING

When food was involved, Sergeant Smelly was a selfish man.

"I think it would be a good idea if you make that Pepperoni, Egg, Chilli and Onion Pizza for me. In case we need my fire-farts to save the day again."

"Normally I wouldn't agree with you Sergeant Smelly, but my executive chef has made you a pizza. He replaced the egg with pickled egg in case we get into a pickle."

"Ooh, an executive chef. Has he got a cool chef's name?"

"Depends what you mean. Is Dai Later-Bitpart a cool chef's name?"

"No, it certainly isn't. He sounds like a Welsh chef who might not last much longer."

Captain Chunder had a plan, but he knew Sergeant Smelly was not going to like it.

"I've got an idea Sergeant Smelly, but you are not going to like it. I've built a rocket that launches you into space where the ozone layer is. The rocket is eco-friendly and is fuelled by fart power. I have been harnessing the power of your farts in my specially designed toilet, which stores the farts you do whilst having a poo. Once in space, you deploy the machine I designed called The Machine that repairs the hole in the ozone layer. You fart into this specially designed fart cannon, then you press the BLUE button which will deploy the depolariser, which will turn your fire-farts into an ozone repairing laser. Now, whatever you do, DO NOT PRESS THIS RED BUTTON."

"This button here that says, if you press this button it will neutralise the reversity and polarity and cause your fire-farts to destroy the ozone layer?" asked Sergeant Smelly.

"Err...yes, that's the one."

"What are my chances of survival?"

"Well, if I'm being honest, not great, but if we record it and put it on YouTube, everyone will see that you repaired the ozone layer and saved the day," said Captain Chunder.

"Again," said Sergeant Smelly.

"Well, if I'm being honest, not great, but if we record it and put it on YouTube, everyone will see that you have repaired the ozone layer and saved the day," repeated Captain Chunder.

"No, I mean save the day…again."

"Ah, I see," said Captain Chunder, followed with a whisper. "You may die trying of course."

"What was the last bit Captain Chunder?"

"I said you'll be a HERO," lied Captain Chunder.

"Where do I sign up?"

"Here, here, here and here," said Captain Chunder producing a contract from his back pocket that protected him in case anything went wrong.

"Something is puzzling me though Captain Chunder. How were you able to invent these incredible machines when you are just a chef?"

"JUST A CHEF!" screamed Captain Chunder. "JUST A CHEF! I went to night school last year and studied a course on Astrophysics and how to build ridiculous machines that will save the world."

"Fair enough, that's good enough for me. Let's get cracking. Which is another good idea. A few cabbage and anchovy omelettes should get some fire-farts brewing nicely. I assume the rocket is designed to bring me back to Earth as well?"

"Err...yes...of course...of course it is Sergeant Smelly," lied Captain Chunder looking the other way so Sergeant Smelly wouldn't see him screwing his face up.

"What are you doing with that screw?" asked Sergeant Smelly.

"Nothing, nothing at all! Oh, one more thing. Whatever you do, and this is the most important thing, don't forget to press the yellow button that will record your day saving antics so we can put it on YouTube. It's called The button that will record your day saving antics so we can put it on YouTube."

"Put it on where? And don't call me a tube!"

"YOUTUBE you tube!"

"I see," lied Sergeant Smelly thinking Captain Chunder was going loopy as he kept repeating himself.

"And what is the rocket called?" asked Sergeant Smelly. "The SMELLY MOBILE perhaps?"

"No, don't be ridiculous. It is called THE OZONE REPAIRER," yelled Captain Chunder jubilantly.

14 EVIL ROCKET LAUNCH

Evil Pumping Pumpkin Man added the finishing touches to the rocket and it looked magnificent. Alas, he immediately knew he would have a problem as Onionman would be desperate to name the rocket. Evil Pumping Pumpkin Man was prepared to stick to his guns. He didn't have any guns, but he was going to stick to them anyway. The rocket would be called DEATH TO THE OZONE and there was absolutely nothing Onionman could do about it.

"How about The Rocket that sends me to the Ozone to destroy the ozone layer?" Onionman was determined to be the namer of all things.

"NO!"

"The Rocket that sends me to the Ozone to destroy the ozone layer because Plan A wasn't working quickly enough?"

"ABSOLUTELY NOT!"

"The Rocket that sends me to the Ozone to use The Machine that puts a hole in the ozone layer and destroys Sergeant Smelly's reputation."

"That does say exactly what we are going to do…but still NO!"

"BOB?"

"Hmm…" said Evil Pumping Pumpkin Man wavering slightly. "It would save on the cost of lettering, and it does have a certain ring to it. YES, I LIKE IT!" he exclaimed. "The Rocket of certain doom for the occupant shall be called BOB!"

"Hang on a minute Pumpy Man. I didn't catch everything you said there. Rocket of certain what?"

"Err…the Rocket of certain Boom. Yes, that's it, the Rocket of certain boom shall be called BOB!" lied Evil Pumping Pumpkin Man getting away with the fact he covered up Onionman's demise. His budget didn't stretch far enough to install the necessary rocket cells for re-entry. He did make an untested spacesuit parachute, but his hopes weren't high. If he managed to escape the rocket and use the parachute, he probably wouldn't make it back in one piece. In fact, there may be a few scientists trying to explain where the large onion meteorite came from.

"So when I get to the ozone layer, I press the DEATH TO THE OZONE button on The Machine that puts a hole in the ozone layer and destroys Sergeant Smelly's reputation."

"Yes."

"Then what?"

"Impending doom!"

"Yay!" exclaimed Onionman. "No wait, impending doom doesn't sound good for me."

"Sorry, I meant impending doom unless you quickly put on the parachute and jump out of BOB!"

"You mean you didn't have enough time to make a rocket that would send me back to Earth?"

"Yes, sorry about that, I used most of the budget on the letters for The Machine that puts a hole in the ozone layer and destroys Sergeant Smelly's reputation," said Evil Pumping Pumpkin Man.

"Oh, that's fair enough I suppose. It is a good name after all," said Onionman. "So this parachute. Will it definitely work?"

"Doubtful," whispered Evil Pumping Pumpkin Man.

"Sorry Evil Pumping Pumpkin Man, I didn't catch that," said Onionman.

"I said without a doubt Onionman. Without a doubt. I'll see you back on Earth in no time at all," lied Evil Pumping Pumpkin Man again.

15 RANDOM CHAPTER 2

Meanwhile, back in the cave, Bunion Man had finally decided what to do. Would he help Onionman or would he get his revenge? The decision had been made.

16 BOB

BOB the rocket blasted off into space with a nervous Onionman aboard.

"TO THE OZONE LAYER AND NOT BEYOND," he shouted hopefully.

He dreamed of flying when he was younger. He dreamed of reaching the stars. But that was before his head turned into an onion. Not that having an onion for a head was going to stop him. It would just make him less aerodynamic and more likely for his onion head to burn up on re-entry. He concentrated on the demise and destruction of Sergeant Smelly's reputation.

"Curse you Sergeant Smelly. I will destroy the ozone layer and you will be blamed for the major destruction that will follow."

As he closed in on the ozone layer, he looked down towards Earth. He saw the awe-inspiring Great Wall of China. He saw the great oceans, a mass of blue covering the globe. He drifted off to a peaceful place where he listened to relaxing classical music and waves rippled gently in the background. It reminded him he used to be a nice person many years ago. He used to have a dog

called Barnaby Chubbles that he would walk
in the park and say hello to all the other nice
people walking their dogs. He remembered
how he was defeated by the power of
Sergeant Smelly's farts and all the nice
thoughts quickly vanished from his head.
With the return of his evil thoughts, he
reached the ozone layer and he prepared
himself to destroy Sergeant Smelly's
reputation.

The spacesuit parachute fitted him
perfectly, as did the specially designed large
onion shaped helmet.

"Say goodbye to your Good Guy
reputation, Sergeant Smelly," said
Onionman pressing the DEATH TO THE
OZONE button. The laser beam shot out
and met the ozone layer, not with a bang,

but with an eerie silence. In that split second, Onionman wondered if he was doing the right thing. His vengeful thoughts altered his agenda from world domination to world destruction. There might not be a world to dominate if this plan worked. He eventually evilled up.

"I AM ONIONMAN. I COME IN EVIL. PREPARE FOR IMPENDING DOOM," said a sombre Onionman as a tear gently rolled down his onion face.

17 BAD NEWS

Back on Earth, major trouble was brewing. Major Trouble was back at the barracks brewing a pot of tea for the soldiers, but that was another story.

Trouble was brewing for Sergeant Smelly and Captain Chunder, as the main headline on the news brought more woes for the less than dynamic duo. The hole in the ozone layer was increasing and they were being blamed. A news reporter standing outside the Institute of Science and Holes in the Ozone and Stuff was reporting on the incident.

"We have recently been informed that the hole in the ozone layer is increasing, which is starting to affect the weather. People are being urged to stay indoors and apply lots of sun cream. Sorry, the people who have been urged to stay indoors and have taken heed, don't necessarily have to apply the sun cream, but they can if they want, especially if they are nipping down to the shops. But the people who have been urged to stay indoors and have not taken heed should definitely apply lots of sun cream. The people who don't know what heed means should also stay indoors," said the reporter outside the Institute of Science and Holes in the Ozone and Stuff. He continued, "The cause of this impending major catastrophe is not, as first thought, Major Catastrophe. It wasn't even Major Destruction. No, I can't believe it myself. But mere months after saving the day and becoming national heroes, Sergeant Smelly and Captain Chunder are the cause of the impending doom. I should remain unbiased because I am a reporter, but hey, the world could be destroyed and it's all the fault of SERGEANT SMELLY AND CAPTAIN CHUNDER. I say we go to Café McPoo and tear them limb…err…I mean we should go to Café McPoo and protest strongly."

18 THE CHUNDER MOBILE

On hearing the news, a group of protesters gathered outside Café McPoo. They chanted songs against Sergeant Smelly and Captain Chunder to show their disapproval.

Sergeant Smelly

Not on your Nelly

Captain Chunder

Oh what a blunder

Sergeant Smelly

You were on the telly

Your farting saved the day

But now you'll make us pay

Captain Chunder

Torn asunder

Your puking saved the day

But now you'll make us pay

The songs went on for literally seconds, before the angry baying crowd ran out of material.

"Sergeant Smelly, we are going to have to launch the rocket now," whispered Captain Chunder so the angry baying crowd wouldn't hear him. He continued, "Sergeant Smelly! Can you hear me?"

"Yes, I can hear you, but we shouldn't be speaking. We don't want to let them know we are here."

"Maybe I shouldn't have left the Open and hiding under the Table sign up on the door," said Captain Chunder.

"Wasn't one of your best signs."

"Anyhoos, we have to launch the rocket now."

"Where is it?" enquired Sergeant Smelly.

"It is around the corner from Onionman's secret lair."

"Seriously?"

"Yes, it was the best wide open space available."

"How are we supposed to get to Onionman's secret lair?"

"Simple. SERGEANT SMELLY…TO THE CHUNDER MOBILE!" whispered Captain Chunder superheroically, as loud as he could whisper.

"Hang on a rude word minute! CHUNDER MOBILE! CHUNDER MOBILE! Surely it should be SMELLY MOBILE. I'm the main character here."

Sergeant Smelly was getting irritated. His name was first. Captain Chunder was Batman's Robin or Mork's Mindy or err…the rubbish one out of some other superhero duos. He wasn't going to stand for it!

"I'm not going to stand for this," said Sergeant Smelly sitting down.

"Whatever Smelly. Stay here with the angry baying crowd if you want. I'm going up to the roof to fly the CHUNDER MOBILE."

"Well, you never said it could fly! I'm right behind you Captain Chunder."

They sneaked up to the secret attic entrance that was created to reach the flat roof that was recently renovated so the CHUNDER MOBILE could fit on top. It was hidden from view in case any angry baying crowds ever gathered at Café McPoo in protest. Sergeant Smelly was impressed. The black surface was glass smooth and his reflection seemed to go on forever. It was polished to perfection. The word

CHUNDER was displayed boldly on the side. And it could fly!

"Awesome," said Sergeant Smelly in some awe. "All it needs is a unicorn horn and it will be perfect. And SMELLY written on the side instead of CHUNDER of course!"

His feeling changed from awe to jealousy in a millisecond.

They stepped inside the CHUNDER MOBILE and it was equally as stunning as the exterior, although there was still no unicorn horn that Sergeant Smelly could see.

"There will definitely be a unicorn horn on the SMELLY MOBILE if Captain Chunder stops being selfish and makes me a superhero mobile," thought Sergeant Smelly to himself.

Captain Chunder started the near silent engine and it purred like a cat getting its belly rubbed. He manoeuvred the CHUNDER MOBILE straight up in the air and they flew off to the launch pad at breakneck speed, almost breaking their necks. When they reached their destination, they jumped out of the CHUNDER MOBILE superheroically and ran to the launch pad. But something was afoot and it wasn't their feet.

19 RELEASE THE FLYING MONKEYS

The celebrations were in full flow as Onionman had returned in one piece. Evil Pumping Pumpkin Man breathed a sigh of relief. His spacesuit parachute actually worked. But they were rudely interrupted. The CCTV outside the secret lair showed the superheroes walking towards their rocket.

"I knew there was something strange about that rocket," said Onionman. "Quickly monions, they are going to launch a rocket that will repair the ozone layer!"

"How do you know?" enquired the monions.

"The name is on the side of the rocket," replied Onionman.

"Ah, we didn't see that," replied the monions feeling rather silly.

"We need to stop them," continued Onionman. "RELEASE THE FLYING MONKEYS!"

"Err…we don't have any flying monkeys Onionman," said Onion Struan.

"RELEASE THE FLYING PTERODACTYLS!"

"Err…Pterodactyls can fly so you don't have to add FLYING," said Onion Struan.

"Yes, okay Onion Struan. RELEASE THE PTERODACTYLS!"

"Err…we don't have any PTERODACTYLS."

"Tread carefully Onion Struan. RELEASE THE FLYING RATS!"

"Err…we don't have any flying rats Onionman."

"Oh for goodness sake. Do we have any evil flying animals at all?"

"Err…no."

"Do we have any flying animals?"

"Err…we have some flying Chihuahuas."

"FLYING CHIHUAHUAS? FLYING CHIHUAHUAS?"

"Err…no just FLYING CHIHUAHUAS."

"Are they evil in anyway?"

"They have an extremely annoying bark and the way their tongues hang out is irksome."

"So, we are going to defeat Sergeant Smelly and Captain Chunder by releasing the slightly irritating Chihuahuas. Is that what you are telling me?"

"Best I can do I'm afraid."

"OKAY, OKAY, RELEASE THE SLIGHTLY IRRITATING FLYING CHIHUAHUAS."

"I SAID, RELEASE THE SLIGHTLY IRRITATING FLYING CHIHUAHUAS."

"Err…we have released them," said Onion Struan.

"But they are just walking about and they aren't even irritating in the slightest. Wait a minute Onion Struan. Those badly constructed wings aren't real are they?"

"Err…no."

"They can't fly, can they?"

"Err…no. We did try training them but their little Chihuahua hearts weren't up for it."

"That's fair enough Onion Struan. Go and have a fifteen minute break and have a ponder and we will address the EVIL FLYING ANIMAL SITUATION LATER."

"Oh, thanks, thanks very much," said a shocked Onion Struan, not noticing the big ball of floating sarcasm hovering in front of his face.

"Goodbye Onion Struan."

Onionman chopped Onion Struan finely and kept the chopped onion in a Tupperware box to make a nice cheese and onion strudel for his supper. Onion Struan was about to become Onion Strudel. All Onionman needed now was some nice cheese.

"Cheese 56, can you come over here for a minute please?"

20 GOOD ROCKET LAUNCH

S ergeant Smelly dodged and weaved through the slightly irritating Chihuahuas and boarded the rocket.

"We have lift off!" confirmed Captain Chunder as one of the slightly irritating non flying Chihuahuas tried to wee on him.

"TO THE OZONE LAYER AND NOT BEYOND," Sergeant Smelly shouted hopefully as the rocket blasted off. He dreamed of flying when he was younger. He dreamed of reaching the stars. As he closed in on the ozone layer, he looked down towards Earth. He saw the awe-inspiring Great Wall of China. He saw the great oceans, a mass of blue covering the globe. He drifted off to a peaceful place where he listened to relaxing classical music and waves rippled gently in the background. He thought to himself, "I wonder how long it will take for my book sales to start rising again." He wasn't one for beautiful scenery or nice sentimental thoughts. All he was interested in was saving the day…to get his book sales back on track.

"I have to put a stop to these evil wrongdoings. Onionman must not be allowed to hamper my book sales...err...I mean...he must not be allowed to destroy the ozone layer. Yeah, that's right. I WILL DEFEAT YOU AGAIN. IN YOUR FACE ONIONMAN."

Sergeant Smelly prepared to fire The Machine that repairs the hole in the ozone layer. He put the spacesuit parachute on, wishing Captain Chunder made it bigger around the waist, but squeezed into it eventually. He had to. His life was at stake. "Mmm...steak," thought Sergeant Smelly hoping for a safe and pleasant return flight. Steak was definitely not on the inflight menu, but when he returned Captain Chunder promised him a slap up meal...

"If you get back..."

"Surely you mean WHEN I get back!" interjected Sergeant Smelly.

"Yes, yes, sorry, I mean WHEN you get back, I will make you a slap up meal with Steak and extra peppercorns and chilli sauce with Cabbage stuffed with Pickled Eggs," lied Captain Chunder.

Back on the rocket, Sergeant Smelly pulled his trousers down, as he felt rumblings in his tummy. It was time to produce the goods. He duly produced several colossal fire-farts into the fart cannon as instructed. He was now ready to press the button on The Machine that repairs the hole in the ozone layer.

"I did put a couple of exclamation marks at the end for emphasis."

"Oh sorry. I didn't see them. So do you want to use the rocket or not?

"Yes, sorry, thank you Evil Pumping Pumpkin Man for making a spare rocket. I will make Sergeant Smelly pay after all. What is the rocket called?" enquired Onionman, clearly thinking of a new name for the rocket.

"BOB 2.0!" replied Evil Pumping Pumpkin Man.

"Can we call it The Rocket..."

"OH SHUT UP ONIONMAN AND GET IN THE ROCKET," yelled Evil Pumping Pumpkin Man.

22 SERGEANT SMELLY IN SPACE

S ergeant Smelly panicked as he could not remember which button he was supposed to press. The fart cannon was locked and loaded and a decision needed made instantly. One wrong button press and he could destroy the universe, never mind the ozone layer. He would produce major destruction leading to major catastrophes. And Major Catastrophe was nowhere to be seen, never mind Major Destruction.

A rocket appeared a quarter of a mile away, which in space still looks about a quarter of a mile away. The name BOB 2.0 was emblazoned on the side of the rocket. Sergeant Smelly looked down at the monitor and zoomed in on BOB 2.0. Onionman appeared at the window.

"UN YAN YAN YAN YAN," laughed Onionman evilly.

"How on earth did you get up here so quickly Onionman?" asked Sergeant Smelly.

"Evil Pumping Pumpkin Man built a spare rocket in case of such situations."

"And how on earth can you hear me?" asked Sergeant Smelly confused.

"We're not on Earth!" said Onionman correcting Sergeant Smelly.

"Oh yes, you are correct. How in space can you hear me? I thought no one could hear you in space."

"They usually can't, but I managed to hack into your communication system even though I have no IT skills whatsoever. Prepare to meet your maker Sergeant Smelly."

"Hi Sergeant Smelly, I'm the author…pleased to meet you," said the author randomly appearing from nowhere.

"Err…hi the author," said Sergeant Smelly a little perplexed as the author disappeared in a puff of randomness.

"And now…prepare to meet Death!"

Onionman pressed a button on the console and a laser shot out and hit the rocket with force. Fortunately, Sergeant Smelly raised the shields just in time and they absorbed the laser. But the shields wouldn't hold out forever.

The force of the laser propelled Sergeant Smelly from one side of the rocket to the other. The shields were down to 1% and the final laser blast collapsed the shields, sending Sergeant Smelly to the console where the buttons were. He remembered just in time that it was the blue button and he raised his hand to press it, but the rocket shook violently again and he landed on one of the buttons. He picked himself up to see which button he had pressed.

"Oh fetid fart fungus!" exclaimed Sergeant Smelly.

23 THIS IS THE END?

Sergeant Smelly had inadvertently pressed the wrong button. The red button. The button Captain Chunder told him not to press. He pressed the button that would neutralise the reversity and polarity and cause his fire-farts to destroy the ozone layer. He pressed the button that was about to destroy the world.

Well he would have done, if the laser from Onionman's rocket hadn't tipped his own rocket 180 degrees and the fire-fart laser from the fart cannon was on its way towards Onionman's rocket. The laser seemed to take forever to reach Onionman's rocket. It appeared to be going in slow motion. He looked down at the console and realised he had also pressed the green button. Underneath the green button was a label that said The button that makes the laser go in slow motion.

He looked down at the monitor and saw Onionman frantically trying to get his spacesuit parachute on. Sergeant Smelly turned around quicker than an out of work celebrity signing up for I'm a Celebrity. He pressed the green button as hard as he could. A warning light came on the dashboard. It said, HITTING THE BUTTON HARD MAKES NO DIFFERENCE WHATSOEVER. PLEASE REFRAIN FROM DOING THIS FOR DRAMATIC EFFECT...THANK YOU!

The fire-fart laser transferred from slow motion to fast motion and accelerated to the rocket that was called BOB 2.0. It instantaneously exploded into a million pieces. Was this the end of Onionman? Was this the end of his evil oniony ways? Would onion space debris float around space forever?

Sergeant Smelly witnessed the explosion on the monitor to his relief. He was back on track to save the day and restore his reputation as a superhero. The only task remaining was to repair the ozone, so he pulled his trousers down once more and attempted to produce a fire-fart into the fart cannon. His fart fuel was running on empty and no fire-fart was forthcoming.

A holograph appeared in front of him. It was Captain Chunder dressed in a hooded bath robe.

"Use the Fridge Norman!" said the holographic Captain Chunder.

Sergeant Smelly could not work out what the hologram was trying to tell him. He thought hard for a couple of minutes and…

"Nope, I got nothing. Wait a minute, perhaps if I grab a drink from the fridge over there right next to the hologram, I'll be able to think clearly. Sergeant Smelly opened

the fridge door and picked up a chilled
bottle of water, which was next to the
Pepperoni, jalapeño and pickled egg pizza.
He gulped down half of the water and
relaxed.

"That's better. I can think clearly now,"
said Sergeant Smelly beginning to think
clearly. "YES, I'VE GOT IT!" shouted
Sergeant Smelly. "Captain Chunder must
have been reminding me to empty the
contents of my fridge at home so the food
doesn't go off. Hoorah! I shall phone my
Auntie Susan and ask her to empty the
contents of my fridge," said Sergeant Smelly.
"No wait," he continued. "It can't be that. I
don't have a fridge. I melted it last week
when I fire-farted in the kitchen. Come to
think of it. I don't have an Auntie Susan

either. And I don't have a phone. Hmm…I shall have to think of something else and I'm feeling peckish. I wonder if Captain Chunder left me anything to eat in the fridge."

And without realising, he finally got the point of the message. He picked up the Pepperoni, jalapeño and pickled egg pizza and scoffed the lot.

"Now where was I?" said Sergeant Smelly. But before he could start thinking again he got the wobbles in his stomach and knew exactly what was about to happen. He ran over to the fart cannon and the fire-fart ripped through his trousers and landed perfectly in the fart cannon. He adjusted the cannon with his butt hanging out his trousers. There was no time to worry about how he looked. He pointed it at the ozone layer and BOOM!

"FIRE-FARTS TO THE RESCUE!"

The laser fired towards the ozone layer in slow motion. And once he stood up and took his huge butt off the green button, the laser fired in fast motion towards the ozone layer. It collided with the ozone layer and the collision of reversed polarity fire-farts and ozone, erupted into a thing of beauty. A hundred billion brightly coloured fartbots repaired the broken universe. A universe broken by power crazed men with voices of authority who spoke to the world and knew they would be listened to. Even though they were lying through their teeth to line their pockets. Well, that and the fact Evil Pumping Pumpkin Man and Onionman created and used a machine to expand the hole that the greedy men had created.

So with his fire-farting caused by a diet to test the bravest of stomachs and bottoms, Sergeant Smelly had saved the day again. Or had he?

24 FORGET SOMETHING?

From out of nowhere, an annoying, dull voice spoke.

"So Sergeant Smelly. You think you have saved the day do you?" said the voice.

Sergeant Smelly jumped at the unexpected voice. He turned around and saw Bunion Man laughing evilly.

"Again," said Sergeant Smelly.

"So Sergeant Smelly. You think you have saved the day do you?"

"No, I meant saved the day…again! Who on earth are you?" exclaimed Sergeant Smelly.

"We are not on Earth."

"Yes, yes, okay, okay…Who in space are you?"

"I am Bunion M…what do you mean who am I. You don't even know who I am? Oh no wait. That's right. We didn't actually meet when you defeated Onionman last time. I AM BUNION MAN. I SPREAD PAIN AND MISERY TO ALL BUNION SUFFERERS OUT THERE."

"Seriously…Bunion Man…pain and misery to all bunion sufferers. What a rock star evil villain you are!" said Sergeant Smelly.

"Well there is no need for that Sergeant Smelly! Anyhoos, as I was saying...so Sergeant Smelly. You think you have saved the day AGAIN do you?"

"Err...yes...I think so."

"And this yellow button here. Was it for anything in particular? You were meant to press it weren't you?"

Sergeant Smelly smacked the base of his hand with his forehead as he realised his schoolboy error. He was supposed to press the yellow button to record himself repairing the ozone layer, but in all the excitement and danger, he forgot to press it. Now no one would know he saved the day.

"Well Sergeant Smelly, you have saved the day, but you haven't saved your reputation, as no one will know. You stupidly forgot to press The button that will record your day saving antics so we can put it on YouTube, you tube," said Bunion Man.

"Yes, it was rather silly wasn't it? Well I guess you and Onionman achieved what you wanted by destroying my superhero reputation. Well done Bunion Man."

"Ha Ha Sergeant Smelly. I fooled you. I was playing with you. I changed sides from evil to good. I pressed the yellow button for you. Recorded the whole lot. Even recorded the slightly irritating flying Chihuahuas in the hope the recording will go viral and I can make some cash."

Sergeant Smelly breathed a sigh of relief. It was definitely looking like he was singlehandedly going to save the day again…with a little help from his friends and a failed villain turned good.

"Thanks muchly Bunion Man," said Sergeant Smelly with a huge 'my book is back in business' smile. "I have to leave now though, as the rocket isn't designed to get back to Earth," continued Sergeant Smelly putting on his spacesuit parachute. He clearly wasn't interested in Bunion Man's safety. He grabbed the camera that recorded the event and jumped out of the rocket, remarkably showing no fear. Well, his book sales were at stake!

25 ESCAPE

Sergeant Smelly rocketed downwards through the atmosphere at 500 mph. He would have been lying if he said he wasn't afraid. He would have been lying if he said he wasn't extremely close to having an accident in his pants, and we're not talking about a fire-farting accident! More of a runny, squelchy accident. Most people would be having a rip-roaring time, but he was too scared to be exhilarated by the event. For him it was a means to get back to Earth. And he was getting back to Earth. Quickly. Too quickly! His spacesuit was beginning to smoulder and he knew he had to get back pronto. He knew he was getting close when he saw the giant onion at Onionman's base. He saw hundreds of monions descending on Captain Chunder and with a quick manoeuvre of his bottom he released a fire-fart, which changed his direction towards the monions. He twisted his body into a ball and smashed into the onion shaped skittles. They softened his landing and he came to a halt at the feet of Captain Chunder.

"Afternoon Captain Chunder. Everything under control here?" asked Sergeant Smelly ever so annoyingly.

"No Sergeant Smelly. Everything is not under control. Evil Pumping Pumpkin Man is in charge of the monions and they are trying to wear me down by throwing rotting cabbages at me. I never thought I would hear myself say this, but I'm covered in cabbage bruises and I smell bad. In fact, I would go as far as to say, I smell like one of your farts."

"We should change your name to Captain Smelly or Captain Cabbages in keeping with the alliteration."

"Oh shut up Smelly. Right, I have an idea. We need to get back to Café McPoo, so you can eat some more fire-farting food. TO THE CHUNDER MOB..."

"Hang on a rude word minute! Didn't we agree it was called the SMELLY MOBILE! I've just been to space and repaired the ozone layer and saved the day. I hurtled back to Earth in a spacesuit parachute at death-defying speed!" insisted Sergeant Smelly.

"Again."

"Hang on a rude word minute! Didn't we agree..." but Captain Chunder stopped him in his tracks.

"Please don't repeat all that again. You know I mean saved the day AGAIN, and NO SMELLY, we didn't agree to change the name. You may have imagined the outcome of the last conversation ended in me changing the CHUNDER MOBILE to the SMELLY MOBILE, but it didn't happen. Perhaps if we get to save the day for a third time, I might build you a SMELLY MOBILE."

"Okay, the next vehicle is definitely the SMELLY MOBILE."

Sergeant Smelly and Captain Chunder raced towards the CHUNDER MOBILE with Sergeant Smelly in a mood.

"Chunder Mobile…hmph!" he whispered to himself. They entered the CHUNDER MOBILE and flew back to Café McPoo without an irritating flying Chihuahua in sight.

26 PREPARING THE FARTING FOOD FEAST

Captain Chunder rushed to the kitchen to prepare some farting fuel for Sergeant Smelly. He needed to prepare a fartastic feast that would make Sergeant Smelly produce wave after wave of fire-farts to destroy the monions and Evil Pumping Pumpkin Man.

"Thank goodness Evil Pumping Pumpkin Man hasn't created a machine like the Onionator that can create hundreds of Pumping Pumpkin minions," thought Captain Chunder.

Back at Onionman's not so secret cave, Evil Pumping Pumpkin Man screamed in delight.

"I'VE GOT IT! I will create a machine like the Onionator that will create hundreds of Pumping Pumpkin minions and I will call them…err…PUMPIONS!" he screamed with the realisation that his evil ingenious idea petered out towards the naming of the Pumping Pumpkin minions.

Back at Café McPoo, Captain Chunder was preparing a feast the customers of Café McPoo would have died for. Not literally died for, as they wouldn't have been able to taste the food. Okay, so Captain Chunder was preparing a feast that the customers of Café McPoo would have enjoyed immensely. He printed a menu out for Sergeant Smelly to peruse...

MENU

Mushroom & jalapeño omelette
with spicy Mexicana cheese

Brussels Sprouts Soup

Haggis, Pepperoni and Baked Bean Pie
with extra jalapeños and Chilli Sauce

Pickled Egg Indaloo Vindaloo

Spicy Baked Beans

Cabbage Soufflé

Sardine and Anchovy wraps
with extra jalapeños

Spicy Beef Empanadas with extra jalapeños

Chilli Macarons with a chocolate chilli filling

Captain Chunder brought out the bottom
burp banquet to Sergeant Smelly's table and
his eyes almost popped out of his head at

the sight of the farting food feast. The slavers slowly trickled down his face as he was salivating so much.

"YUUUUUUUUUUUMMMMMMM!" drooled Sergeant Smelly on to the table.

"Captain Chunder, you are a culinary genius."

It was Sergeant Smelly against food and he was determined he was going to win.

And he did.

"Right, let's go Smelly. We have a job to do. We have to stand up for everyone's rights. The right not to be terrorized by evil men who had vegetable accidents. We have to stand up and tell them it's not okay to take their bad luck out on everyone else. We have to stand up to the cowardly bullies and their cowardly followers. We have to say;

IT IS NOT OKAY TO BE BAD.

IT IS NOT OKAY TO BE
VENGEFUL.

IT IS NOT OKAY TO BE BITTER
AND TWISTED.

IT IS NOT OKAY TO LIVE FOR
REVENGE.

IT IS NOT OKAY TO BE A TROLL.

IT IS NOT OKAY TO BE EVIL.

Don't you agree Sergeant Smelly?"

"Sorry, what did you say?" said Sergeant
Smelly who wasn't listening. "I was eating
these peppery after dinner mints you made.
They are the best peppery after dinner mints
I have ever tasted. They are the only
peppery after dinner mints I have tasted and
henceforth the best peppery after dinner

mints I have ever tasted. Sorry, what was it you were saying?"

"Oh never mind Smelly. No one will remember the speech anyway with all the fire-farting going on," said Captain Chunder feeling a sense of moral futility.

"I think we better go Chunder before…"

"You can't Chunder now. You'll never be able to produce the fire-farts. And chundering is my job!" interrupted Captain Chunder.

"I hadn't finished…I think we better go, CAPTAIN Chunder, before I explode. I feel like a walking fire-fart bomb that could go off any second."

And off they went fearlessly…well, Captain Chunder went fearlessly. Sergeant

Smelly followed tentatively a few steps behind.

"TO THE SMELLY MOBILE!" shouted Sergeant Smelly.

"Don't even go there, Smelly. It's got CHUNDER written on the side and it's not coming off. So what is it?"

"Okay, okay, to the Chunder Mobile," Sergeant Smelly said miserably.

"No, with emphasis please," said Captain Chunder taking charge.

"Okay, TO THE CHUNDER MOBILE!"

27 BATTLEGROUND

The CHUNDER MOBILE arrived at Onionman's not so secret cave. The superheroes were prepared for the final battle. Evil Pumping Pumpkin Man sat on a horse with his troops behind him prepared for a medieval battle with a pumpkin surprise. There were hundreds of pumpkins with small arms and legs, with various badly carved pumpkin faces. All the faces were unique and evil, apart from one. When Evil Pumping Pumpkin Man tested the machine, he forgot to switch on the random evil face generator, and the outcome was an insanely happy pumping pumpkin. He brandished a weapon like the other pumpkins, but less menacing. Well, not menacing at all really. But apart from Shiny Happy Pumpkin brandishing a stick in a non evil kind of way…there were hundreds of evil pumpkins prepared for pumpkin evilness.

"Sergeant Smelly, did you bring the chair that spins around really fast?"

"Err…no."

"Why not?" enquired Captain Chunder.

"Err…I sold it to a fan on eBay."

"His name wasn't Johnny Pumpkin was it?"

"Err...yes...is that bad?"

"Well yes, yes it is Sherlock. Don't worry Sergeant Smelly. I brought the fart cannon from the rocket and made a few modifications so we can fart those onions and pumpkins to kingdom come."

"Where is kingdom come?" enquired Sergeant Smelly.

"It's over there. Next to the bomb factory," replied Captain Chunder.

"Oh yes, so it is. Didn't the fart cannon burn up in the atmosphere along with the rocket?"

"Err...no...I had a shield generator around it, so it would come back to Earth intact."

"Good idea, I think we should hurry up though. I'm not sure I can keep these farts in much longer," said Sergeant Smelly clenching his buttocks. But before they could set up the fart cannon they heard loud shouting and screaming behind them.

"Aaaaaaarrrrrrrrrrrgggggggggggghhhhhhh," screamed the pumpkins who were catapulted from The Chair that spins around really fast towards them. They were screaming for two reasons. The first because they were being thrown high and fast…and the second because they really were pumping pumpkins, as Evil Pumping Pumpkin Man made them in his image. As they were falling down towards the superheroes, they fire-farted towards them. Which were equally painful to them as they were to anyone who got in their way. Or they would have been, if Sergeant Smelly and Captain Chunder hadn't dodged them.

"Quickly Sergeant Smelly, run over to that small wall in the middle of nowhere that looks like it shouldn't be there, so we can hide behind it and load the fart cannon with the power of your farts."

They ran over and hid behind the wall, dodging the flying fire-farting pumpkins along the way.

Sergeant Smelly dropped his trousers again and released the loudest and longest pants parter ever heard. If only someone from the Guinness Book of Records was there. It would have certainly been a record breaker, as well as a trouser breaker. And it wasn't just one. The fart power feast was causing Sergeant Smelly to produce multiple trouser trumpets and the fart cannon was close to capacity in no time.

"We need to use the fart cannon quickly Captain Chunder, before it overloads and sends us all to kingdom come."

"You'll have to stop producing the farting goods Smelly."

"It doesn't have an off switch I'm afraid. I ate one too many mouthfuls of the Pickled Egg Indaloo Vindaloo. No, wait…I think it's stopping now. Thank goodness. My butt cheeks are red raw and I don't think they could have taken any more fire."

"Okay, jump off and we'll line up the cannon."

They moved out from their hiding place and aimed the fart cannon towards Evil

Pumping Pumpkin Man and his evil vegetable troops and Shiny Happy Pumpkin. It was a shame to defeat his shiny happy little pumpkin face.

Evil Pumping Pumpkin Man started up the chair that spins around really fast and catapulted another thirty fire-farting pumpkins towards them. But this time they were ready. The pumpkins came hurtling towards them at 100 mph and it looked like impending pumpkin shaped doom for our superhero duo. Was this the end of our dynamic duo? Not if Captain Chunder had anything to do with it and he pressed the green button.

"LET THE POWER OF FART COMMENCE!" yelled Captain Chunder superheroically.

"Err…don't you think I should have shouted that line Captain Chunder," enquired Sergeant Smelly.

"Possibly, but I don't think anyone would have heard you from your cowering position behind the wall. And in the future, when you are telling your fans this story, you will probably say you said it anyway," said Captain Chunder, not caring either way.

"True enough. But I have a new catchphrase and it will look good on a t-shirt…FIRE-FARTS TO THE RESCUE!"

The laser fired towards the pumpkins and caught them all in its lasery grip and moved them slowly back to Evil Pumping Pumpkin Man. When the pumpkins were in line with Evil Pumping Pumpkin Man, Captain

Chunder shouted, "Now Sergeant Smelly, press the green button."

He pressed the green button and the pumpkins were released, and flew towards Evil Pumping Pumpkin Man and the monions in fast motion. The pumpkins were on fire and they hit Evil Pumping Pumpkin Man and hundreds of the others, knocking them out instantly. Captain Chunder quickly fired the fart cannon again as the other monions and pumpions were advancing on them, but the fart cannon was fully loaded. They had no chance to avoid the stream of fire-fart lasers. Those who did survive ran away to the field behind them. Unfortunately for them, it was the annual Explode a Pumpkin day in the field, and hundreds of pumpkin exploding enthusiasts blew up the remaining pumpkins into a million pumpkin pieces.

Back on the battleground, a victorious Sergeant Smelly and Captain Chunder looked around for bystanders praising them for saving the day.

"Isn't this the part when everyone tells us how awesome we are Captain Chunder?"

"Usually. Did you post the video to YouTube to show we were innocent?"

"OH POOP! CAPTAIN CHUNDER...TO THE CHUNDER MOBILE!"

28 SAVING THE DAY

Sergeant Smelly and Captain Chunder ran back to the CHUNDER MOBILE. They saved the day from evil once again, but no one witnessed it. They returned to Café McPoo and uploaded the video, so the whole world could see that Onionman and Evil Pumping Pumpkin Man were to blame for making the hole in the ozone layer increase and Sergeant Smelly repaired the hole. Millions of people around the world watched the videos and realised the superheroes were set up. Most importantly for Sergeant Smelly - the website that gave the recipes away free was closed down.

"Hooray for Sergeant Smelly and Captain Chunder. They have saved the day," shouted millions of people around the world at the same point in time.

"Again," said Sergeant Smelly.

"Hooray for Sergeant Smelly and Captain Chunder. They have saved the day."

"No, no, no! Hooray for Sergeant Smelly and Captain Chunder. They have saved the day AGAIN!"

"Ah, we see now," they shouted in unison. "Hooray for Sergeant Smelly and Captain Chunder. They have saved the day AGAIN!"

29 THIS IS THE END?

In an ocean far, far away, a man with a burnt spacesuit and an onion for a head, sat in a dinghy bobbing up and down on the water.

"Never mind," said Bunion Man folding his spare spacesuit parachute away neatly. There's always tomorrow."

"Oh shut up Bunion Man!"

THE END

Thank you indeedly for reading this book.

I hope you enjoyed it, and if you wouldn't mind, could you please leave a review.

Thanks muchly.

See you soon and may the farts be with you!

Sergeant Smelly

ABOUT THE AUTHOR

James Sharkey was born in Hobbiton in the Shire before being expelled for being too tall.

He was transported to the real world in Fife in Scotland, where he currently lives alone with his partner and son.

He is currently writing the 7th book in the amazing Sergeant Smelly & Captain Chunder series which will be out in 2015.

Other books by James Sharkey

Sergeant Smelly and Captain Chunder Save The Day

Sergeant Smelly and Captain Chunder: Lost in Time

Sergeant Smelly and Captain Chunder: Dimensions

A Sergeant Smelly Christmas

Sergeant Smelly and Captain Chunder: Aliens

Sergeant Smelly And Captain Chunder Save The Day Audio Book

Coming Soon in 2015

Sergeant Smelly and Captain Chunder: Aliens Revenge

www.sergeantsmelly.co.uk

Printed in Great Britain
by Amazon